DATE DUE

16149

SCHWA-
RTZ

Schwartz, Amy.

The lady who put
salt in her coffee.

DISCARD

THE LADY WHO PUT SALT IN HER COFFEE

16149

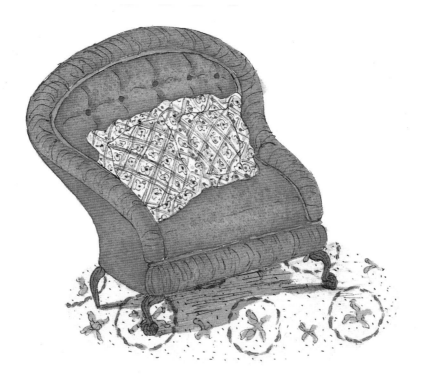

from "The Peterkin Papers" by

Lucretia Hale

adapted and illustrated by

Amy Schwartz

Harcourt Brace Jovanovich, Publishers

San Diego   New York   London

Requests for permission to make copies of any
part of the work should be mailed to:
Copyrights and Permissions Department,
Harcourt Brace Jovanovich, Publishers,
Orlando, Florida 32887.

Library of Congress Cataloging-in-Publication Data
Schwartz, Amy.
The lady who put salt in her coffee: from the Peterkin
papers by Lucretia Hale/adapted and illustrated by
Amy Schwartz.
p. cm.
Summary: When Mrs. Peterkin accidentally puts salt
in her coffee, the entire family embarks on an elaborate
quest to find someone to make it drinkable again.
ISBN 0-15-243475-5
[1. Humorous stories.]   I. Hale, Lucretia P. (Lucretia
Peabody), 1820–1900.   Peterkin papers.   II. Title.
PZ7.S406Lad 1989
[E]—dc19   88-15725

First edition
A B C D E

The illustrations in this book were done in
watercolor and pen and ink on Rives BFK paper.
The text type was set in Horley Old Style by
Thompson Type, San Diego, California.
Printed and bound by Tien Wah Press, Singapore
Production supervision by Warren Wallerstein
and Eileen McGlone
Designed by Nancy J. Ponichtera

AUTHOR'S NOTE
"The Lady Who Put Salt in Her
Coffee" by the American author
Lucretia P. Hale (1820–1900) was
first published in Our Young Folks
magazine in 1867. It was the first of
what grew to be a collection of more
than 30 stories, "The Peterkin
Papers."

Minimal editing was necessary to
adapt the original text to the
picturebook format: I have deleted a
few sentences and phrases and
modified some transitions, but the
language is Lucretia P. Hale's
throughout.

FOR BECKY, DEBBIE, AND JOAN

*T*his was Mrs. Peterkin. It was a mistake. She had poured out a delicious cup of coffee, and, just as she was helping herself to cream, she found she had put in salt instead of sugar!

It tasted bad.

What should she do? Of course she couldn't drink the coffee; so she called in the family. The family came in; they all tasted, and looked, and sat down to think.

At last Agamemnon, who had been to college, said, "Why don't we ask the advice of the chemist?"

Mrs. Peterkin said, "Yes," and Mr. Peterkin said, "Very well." So the little boys put on their india-rubber boots, and off they went.

The chemist was just trying to find something that would turn everything it touched into gold. He had a large glass bottle into which he put all kinds of gold and silver, and many other valuable things, and melted them over the fire till he had almost found what he wanted. He could turn things into almost-gold. But he had used up all the gold that he had around the house. He had used up his wife's gold thimble and his great-grandfather's gold-bowed spectacles, and he had melted the gold head of his great-great-grandfather's cane. He was just now down on his knees before his wife, asking her to let him have her wedding ring to melt with all the rest.

His wife was just consenting when the Peterkin family burst in. You can imagine how mad the chemist was! He came near throwing his crucible — that was the name of his melting pot — at their heads. But he didn't. He listened as calmly as he could to the story of how Mrs. Peterkin had put salt in her coffee.

At first he said he couldn't do anything about it, but when Agamemnon said they would pay in gold, he packed up his bottles in a leather case and went back with them all.

First he looked at the coffee, and then he stirred it. He put in a little chlorate of potassium and the family tried it all around, but it tasted no better. Then he stirred in a little bichlorate of magnesia.

Mrs. Peterkin didn't like that. "I have it!" said the chemist.
"A little ammonia is just the thing!"
But no, it wasn't the thing at all.

Then he tried, each in turn, some oxalic, phosphoric, chloric, hyperchloric, sulphuric, boracic, silicic, nitric, and carbonic acid. Mrs. Peterkin tasted each. "The flavor is pleasant," she said, "but not precisely that of coffee."

So he tried a little calcium, aluminum, barium, and strontium and half of a third of a sixteenth of a grain of arsenic. This gave rather a pretty color, but still Mrs. Peterkin said ungratefully, "It tastes of anything but coffee."

The chemist said that what he had done ought to have taken out the salt. The theory remained the same, although the experiment had failed. He should like to be paid and go.

But there was the coffee! All sat and thought a while, till Elizabeth Eliza asked, "Why don't we go to the herb woman?" Now the herb woman was an old woman who came round to sell herbs and knew a great deal. They all shouted with joy at the idea of asking her. So the boys put on their india-rubber boots again, and they set off.

It was a long walk through the village, but they came at last to
the herb woman's house at the foot of a high hill. They went
through her little garden.

Here she had marigolds and hollyhocks, and old maids and tall sunflowers, and all kinds of sweet-smelling herbs, so that the air was full of tansy tea and elder blow.

They went into a small parlor, which smelt very spicy. All around hung little bags full of catnip, and peppermint, and other kinds of herbs; and dried stalks hung from the ceiling.

But there was no little old woman.

She had gone up into the woods, so Elizabeth Eliza, Agamemnon, Solomon John, and the little boys thought they would follow her. They had to climb up over high rocks and in among huckleberry bushes and blackberry vines—but the little boys had their india-rubber boots. At last they discovered the little old woman digging with her trowel around a sassafras bush. (They knew her by her hat.)

They told her their story—how their mother had put salt in her coffee, and how the chemist had made it worse instead of better, and how their mother couldn't drink it. Wouldn't she come and see what she could do? And she said she would and took up her little old apron with pockets filled with everlasting and penny-royal, and went back to her house.

She took some tansy and peppermint, spearmint and cloves, pennyroyal and sweet marjoram, wild thyme and some of the other time—such as you have in clocks—sappermint and oppermint, catnip, valerian, and hop; indeed, there isn't a kind of herb you can think of that the little old woman didn't have.

Meanwhile Mrs. Peterkin was getting quite impatient for her coffee.

As soon as the little old woman came she set the coffee over the fire. First she put in a little hop for the bitter. But Mrs. Peterkin said, "It tastes like hop tea and not at all like coffee."

Then she tried a little flagroot and snakeroot, then some spruce gum, some rue and rosemary, some sweet marjoram and sour, some wild thyme and some of the tame time, and catnip and valerian.

The children tasted after each mixture, but made dreadful faces. Mrs. Peterkin tasted, and did the same. The more the old woman put in, the worse it seemed to taste.

So the old woman shook her head, and muttered a few words, and said she must go. She believed the coffee was bewitched. All she would take for pay was five cents in currency.

The family was in despair. It was growing late in the day, and Mrs. Peterkin hadn't had her cup of coffee. At last Elizabeth Eliza said, "They say that the lady from Philadelphia, who is staying in town, is very wise. Suppose we go and ask her what is best to be done." To this they all agreed. It was a great thought.

And off they went.

Elizabeth Eliza told the lady from Philadelphia the whole story — how her mother had put salt in the coffee; how the chemist had been called in; how he tried everything but could make it no better; and how they went for the little old herb woman; and how she had tried in vain, for her mother still couldn't drink the coffee. The lady from Philadelphia listened very attentively.

Then she said, "Why doesn't your mother make a fresh cup of coffee?" Elizabeth Eliza started with surprise. Solomon John shouted with joy; so did Agamemnon; so did the little boys. "Why didn't we think of that?" said Elizabeth Eliza.

They all went back to their mother . . .

. . . and she had her cup of coffee.

The Self-Made Snowman

by Fernando Krahn

J. B. Lippincott Company/Philadelphia and New York

U.S. Library of Congress Cataloging in Publication Data
Krahn, Fernando.
The self-made snowman.
SUMMARY: Knocked off the cliff by a mountain sheep, a clump of snow rolls down the mountain
gradually taking the appearance of an enormous and well-dressed snowman.
[1. Stories without words. 2. Snow—Fiction] I. Title.
PZ7.K8585Se   [E]   74-551   ISBN-0-397-31472-8

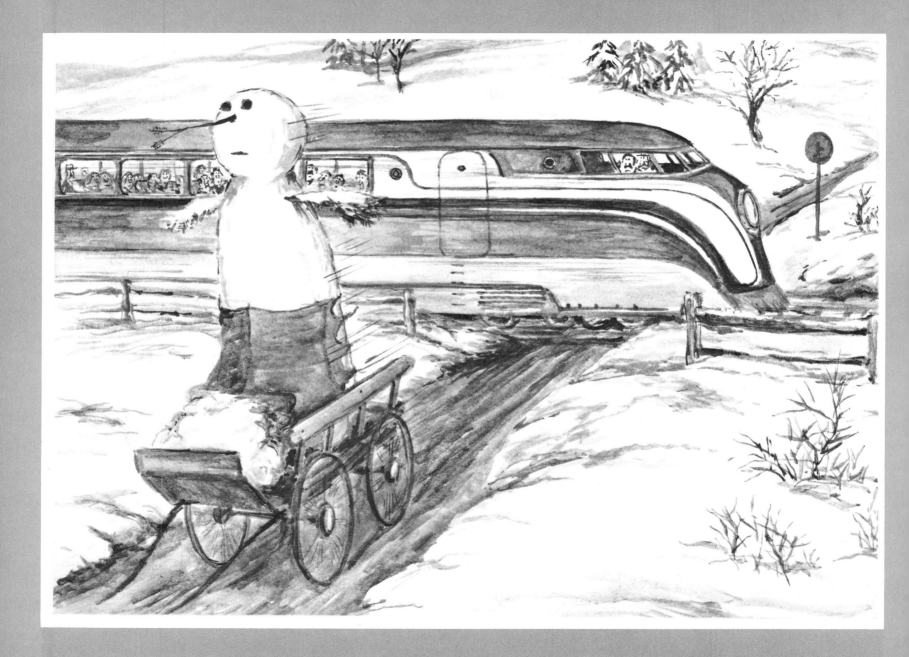

FERNANDO KRAHN, who was born in Chile, has been drawing since he was a little boy. Especially, he says, "I enjoyed making humorous illustrations of public catastrophes." While *The Self-Made Snowman* is hardly a public catastrophe, it certainly reflects Krahn's appreciation for the unusual and the ludicrous in human and animal affairs. Author and/or illustrator of more than fifteen books (most recently *Hardlucky* by Miriam Chaikin), Krahn is also a well-known cartoonist and received a Guggenheim Foundation Fellowship in 1973 to create new film animation methods. He, his wife (co-author of two books), and their three children live in Santiago, Chile, when they aren't traveling.